A VISIT TO MOSCOW

Adapted by Anna Olswanger
from a story by
Rabbi Rafael Grossman

Illustrated by Yevgenia Nayberg

In memory of Rabbi Rafael Grossman,
with thanks to Aviva, Hillel, Shamai, Shukie
and the late Shirley Zaretsky Grossman —A.O.

To my parents. —Y.N.

Library of Congress Cataloging-in-Publication Data

Names: Olswanger, Anna, 1953- author. | Grossman, Rafael G. | Nayberg, Yevgenia, illustrator.
Title: A visit to Moscow / adapted by Anna Olswanger from a story by Rabbi Rafael Grossman ; illustrated by Yevgenia Nayberg.
Description: Berkeley, CA : West Margin Press, [2022] | Summary: "An American rabbi enters Soviet Russia to investigate reports of persecution among the Jewish community. Though heavily monitored once he enters the state, one day the rabbi manages to sneak away in a taxi and discovers a secret that will change his life forever"-- Provided by publisher.
Identifiers: LCCN 2021050712 (print) | LCCN 2021050713 (ebook) | ISBN 9781513128733 (hardback) | ISBN 9781513128740 (ebook)
Subjects: CYAC: Graphic novels. | Rabbis--Fiction. | Jews--Russia--Fiction. | LCGFT: Historical comics. | Graphic novels.
Classification: LCC PZ7.7.O428 Vis 2022 (print) | LCC PZ7.7.O428 (ebook) | DDC 741.5/973--dc23/eng/20211110
LC record available at https://lccn.loc.gov/2021050712
LC ebook record available at https://lccn.loc.gov/2021050713

Printed in China
26 25 24 23 22 1 2 3 4 5

Published by
WEST
MARGIN
PRESS
WestMarginPress.com

Proudly distributed by Ingram Publisher Services

WEST MARGIN PRESS
Publishing Director: Jennifer Newens
Marketing Manager: Alice Wertheimer
Project Specialist: Micaela Clark
Editor: Olivia Ngai
Design & Production: Rachel Lopez Metzger

Whoever saves a single life is considered to have saved the whole world.

Mishnah Sanhedrin 4:9

Zev looks down at stone cliffs.

He sees ruins of a rampart resting on a hill.

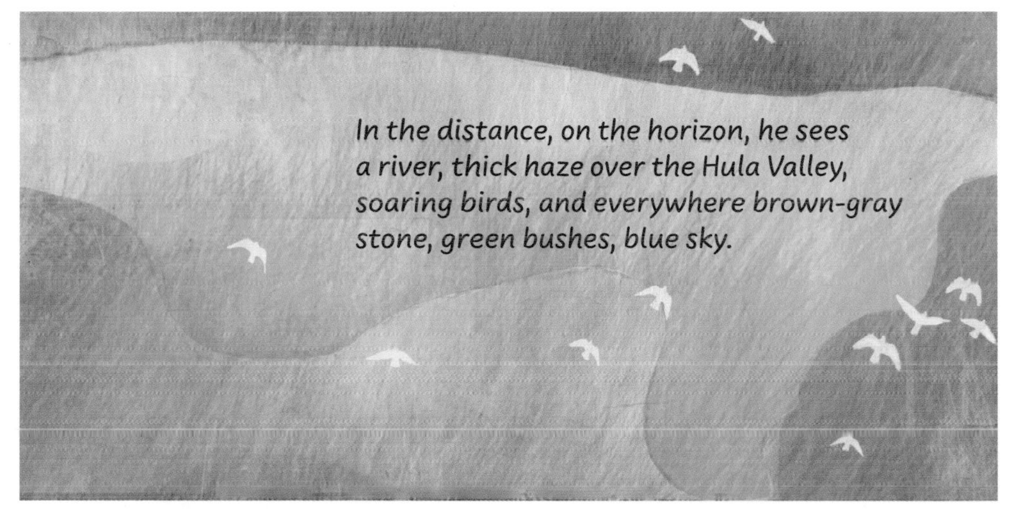
In the distance, on the horizon, he sees
a river, thick haze over the Hula Valley,
soaring birds, and everywhere brown-gray
stone, green bushes, blue sky.

He's looking down from heaven, he's sure of it.

Then the stone, the dirt, the bushes vanish. Zev hovers over his body. He feels cold and wants to rub his arms.

He tries to remember his name, but can't. A voice draws him through the shadows. Zev discovers he can move.

A man sits at the head of a crowded table.
He lifts a knife and cuts into a loaf of bread.

Jagged chunks spread out in front of him.

Crumbs scatter.

The man sits back
in his chair.

His voice draws Zev closer.
Zev can make out one word.

Moscow

SUMMER OF 1965

We were a group of
rabbis from America.

We had been sent to
meet with Soviet Jews.

We wanted to find out if
what we had heard was
true. That the Jews lived
in fear of being reported
to the KGB for public acts
of Judaism. That they
were watched. Followed.
That some Jews were
even arrested.

We were standing in the lobby of the Metropol Hotel when the Intourist bus arrived.
This afternoon you visit our famous Red Square.

I'm sorry, but I have a headache.

It was a lie, of course.
I asked to stay behind in my room.
INTOURIST

After the other rabbis left in the bus for Red Square, I walked outside.
Intourist
I found what I was looking for.
A taxi.

I showed the driver the return address on the envelope.

As we drove through the streets, I studied the rows of gray, wooden buildings, all one story. The buildings looked like boxes.

I didn't see any street signs, so I had no idea if the mud and gravel street where the taxi driver stopped was the street where Meyer Gurwitz lived.

I pointed to the return address on the envelope.
Are you sure this is the right street? Where's number 35?
T

I pulled a few paper rubles from my pocket and held them out to the driver. He reached over the seat and took them.

Spasibo.

I got out of the taxi and started to cross the muddy yard in front of me.
But what if Meyer Gurwitz doesn't live here anymore?

The driver had already started the motor.
I watched him drive away.

35
Slowly I made my way through the mud to a wooden building with "35" painted on it.

I looked again at the letter from Meyer Gurwitz to his sister Bela.

I walked through a small hallway.

I found number 4, but I didn't see a bell to ring.

I became nervous and worried how I would get back to Moscow and the Metropol Hotel. Why didn't anyone answer?

I spoke to him in Yiddish. I knew from Bela that he would understand.
You're Meyer Gurwitz? Bela's brother?
Niet zdes nikakovo Meyera.

I'm sorry, I don't speak Russian. I'm here to see you for just a few minutes. I left my hotel without my tour guide's permission.

The man stepped into the hall and closed the door behind him. He wore a frayed brown suit and, despite the summer heat, a wool cap.

There's no Meyer Gurwitz here.
This time, he spoke to me in Yiddish, but I heard a quiver in his voice. Was he afraid?

You don't have to pretend anything with me. I'm a rabbi, a friend of your sister's in New York.

I knew I didn't look like a rabbi. Old-style rabbis wore long black coats and black hats. They had long beards.

I quoted from Pirkei Avot.

Al tistakel bakankan elah bemah sheyesh bo.
"Don't look at the jug but at what it contains."

A second passed—the man barely nodded.

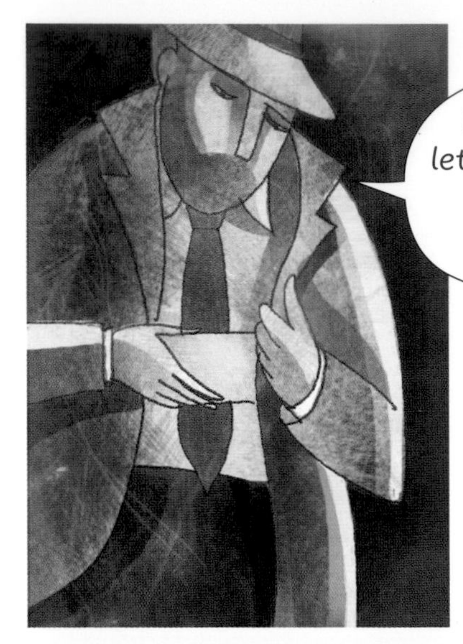

I have your last letter to your sister. I think it's over ten years old.

How did you get this?

Bela gave it to me. She read in the newspaper that I was traveling to the Soviet Union as part of a rabbinical delegation.

She told me that she was worried because she hadn't heard from you for over ten years.
She made me promise to try to find you. You're Bela's brother, aren't you?

He hesitated. I could tell that he didn't trust me.
Look, if I worked for the KGB, would I talk to you in Yiddish?

I know Jews who work for the KGB and speak Yiddish.

I'd been told that in America. Now I wasn't sure what to say. I wished I had asked Bela to write a letter to Meyer to explain who I was.
Please, let me come in. Your sister only wants to know if you have a bed to sleep in and food to eat—

Meyer Gurwitz stepped back.
I was afraid he was about to slam the door of his apartment in my face.

I told you, I'm not
the KGB. You don't have
to hide from me.

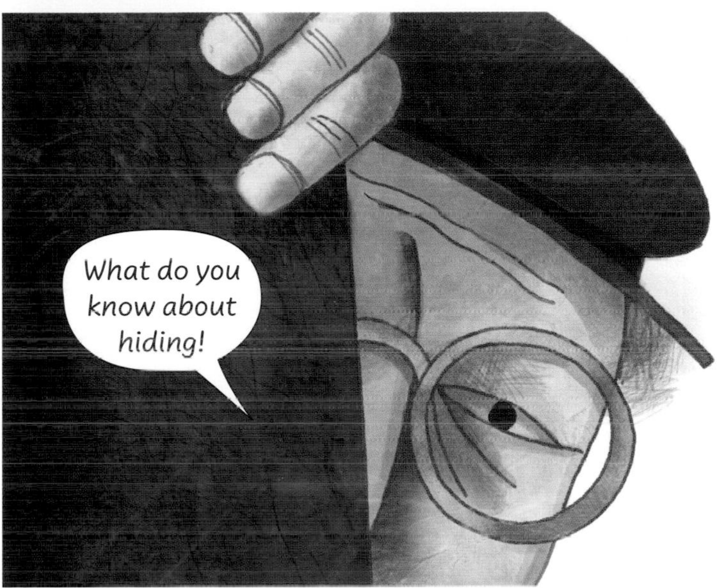
What do you
know about
hiding!

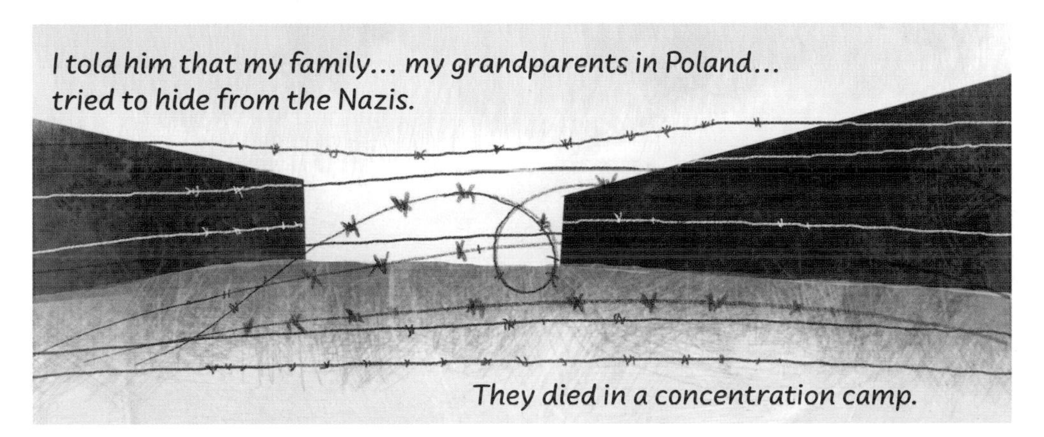
I told him that my family... my grandparents in Poland...
tried to hide from the Nazis.
They died in a concentration camp.

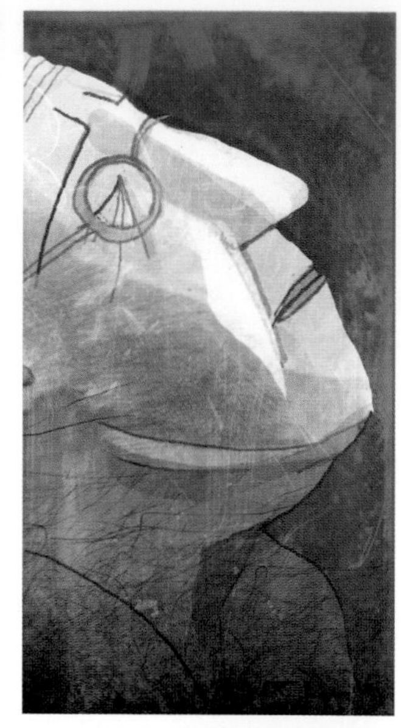

Meyer looked down at the wooden floor.

I'll be gone someday, and then what happens to him?
What happens to who?
Swear to me never to tell anyone in the Soviet Union what you will see inside my home.
I swear.
But he didn't move.
I swear by the Torah.

3
4
5

I saw a bed along the left wall. A woman, who didn't look at me or at Meyer, stood in front of the bed and looked at the floor. She wore a brown head scarf as frayed as Meyer's suit.

Meyer introduced me in a low voice.
My wife.
I smiled at the woman. She smiled back at the floor.

I could make out another bed along the right wall, a small window, a shelf with a large metal pitcher, a large pan, dishes and pots, and, in the corner between the shelf and the bed, a heavy curtain. I thought the curtain might be part of a closet.

Meyer asked me to sit down. I sat in one wooden chair, and he and his wife sat in the other two chairs around a table in the center of the room.

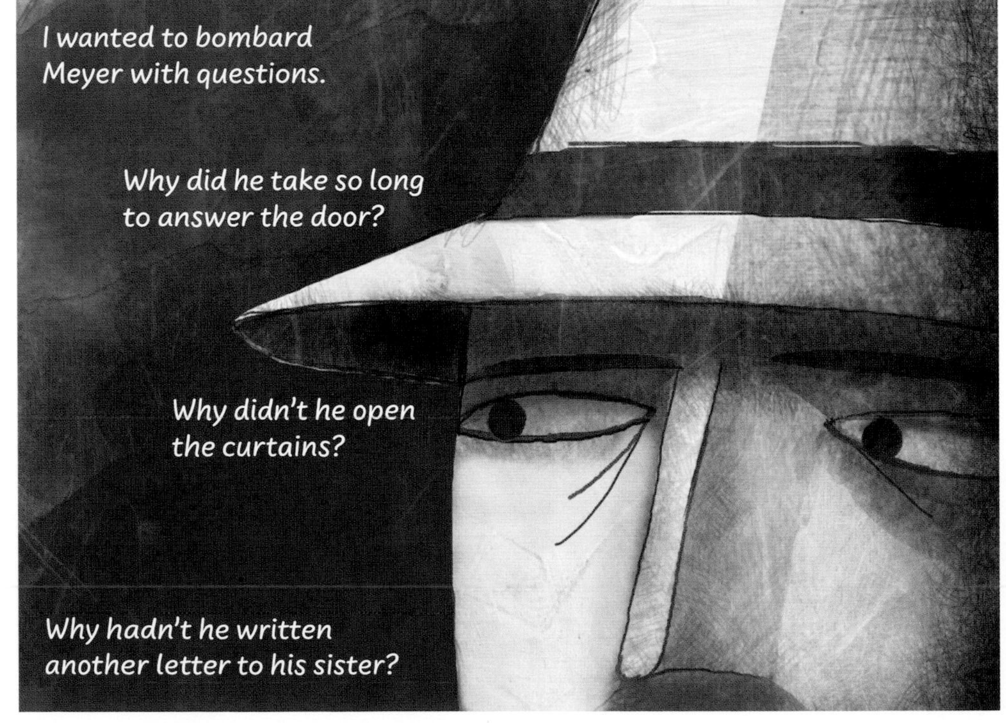
I wanted to bombard Meyer with questions.
Why did he take so long to answer the door?
Why didn't he open the curtains?
Why hadn't he written another letter to his sister?

Bella says you're an engineer. How long have you been working in Moscow?
Since after the war. I wasn't married then. The Ministry of Building brought me here.

I didn't want to go back to the town where we were born, so I didn't care.

You and...?

Bela. Zev, too.

Meyer glanced behind him.

Perhaps you would like some tea?
Yes.

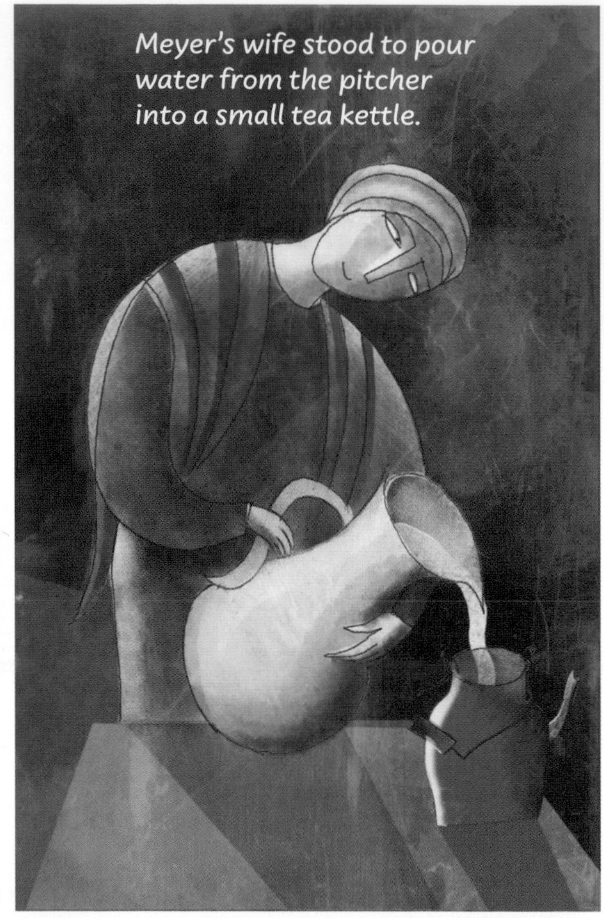
Meyer's wife stood to pour water from the pitcher into a small tea kettle.

As she lit the gas burner, I thought I saw a ripple in the heavy curtain next to her.
I stared at the curtain and saw the ripple again.

Remember, you swore.
Then Meyer turned and called softly to the ripple.

It's all right, Zov, you can come out.

This is my son.

I smiled at the young boy. Meyer must have named him after his brother Zev.
Hello, Zev.
This is a rabbi from America.

From America?

Yes.

A real rabbi?

Of course. Haven't you ever seen a rabbi before?

Zev laughed as he shook his head.

Didn't you ever walk by a shul and peek inside?

I've never seen a synagogue.

But how do you learn about being a Jew? Does your father send you to one of the underground schools?

I don't go to school.

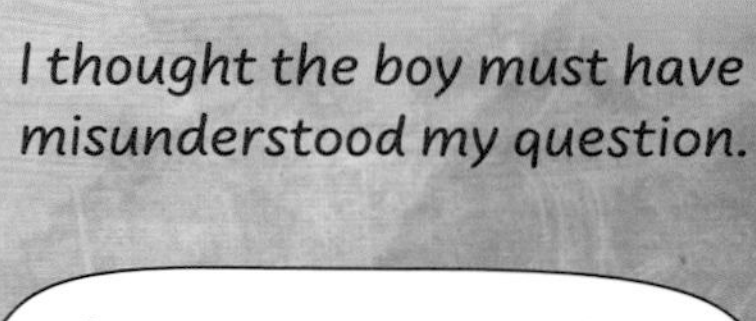
I thought the boy must have misunderstood my question.
Of course you go to school. Every child does. You're in the third grade, I bet.

I've never been to school.

He's never been out of this room.

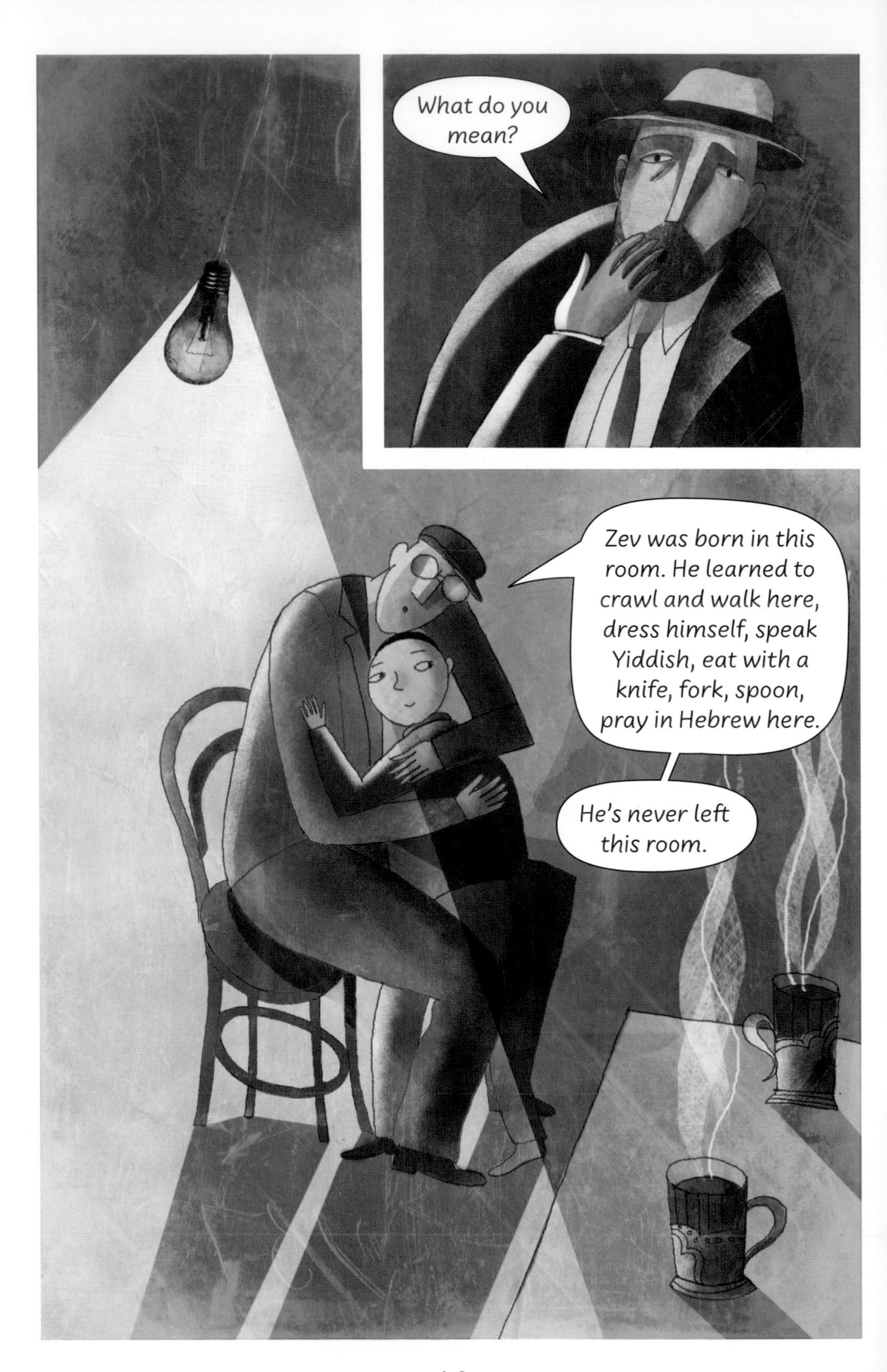
What do you mean?
Zev was born in this room. He learned to crawl and walk here, dress himself, speak Yiddish, eat with a knife, fork, spoon, pray in Hebrew here.
He's never left this room.

I couldn't believe what I was hearing.
Was it possible the little boy had never been outside?
But... why?

Meyer stroked his son's head.
His eyes never left mine.
Because we are Jews.
Because Zev is a Jew, and because my son can remain a Jew only as long as he remains in this room.

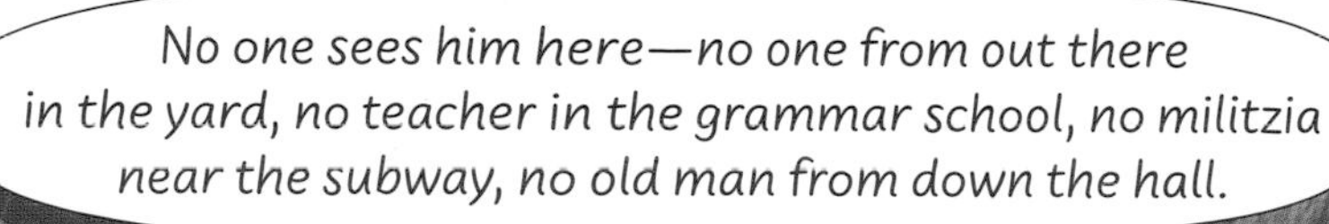
No one sees him here—no one from out there in the yard, no teacher in the grammar school, no militzia near the subway, no old man from down the hall.

M

No one calls Zev "zhid." No one yanks his yarmulke from his head. No one teaches him arithmetic and the Russian language on the Jewish Sabbath, or feeds him milk with meat from a state school lunch.
No one laughs at him because he prays to God.

But... don't you want him to walk outside and see the stars, like our father Abraham in the Torah?
Through the window, Zev looks out at night. We turn off all the lights so that no one can see us from the street. Then we open the curtains and unlock the window.
Zev leans out and feels the wind on his face. He looks at the moon and the stars.

The moon doesn't belong to the Soviets. Neither do the stars. Zev loves the moon and stars because they belong to God.

For a moment, I considered taking Zev's hand and running with him into the hall.
But what would I do with the pale boy who had never been outside the room he was born in?

Meyer—
I'll take you to the bus stop. Your tour guide must be looking for you.

Is it true... that in Israel children go to school and learn Torah?

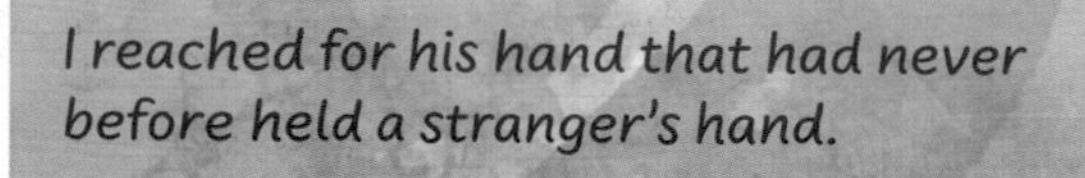
I reached for his hand that had never before held a stranger's hand.

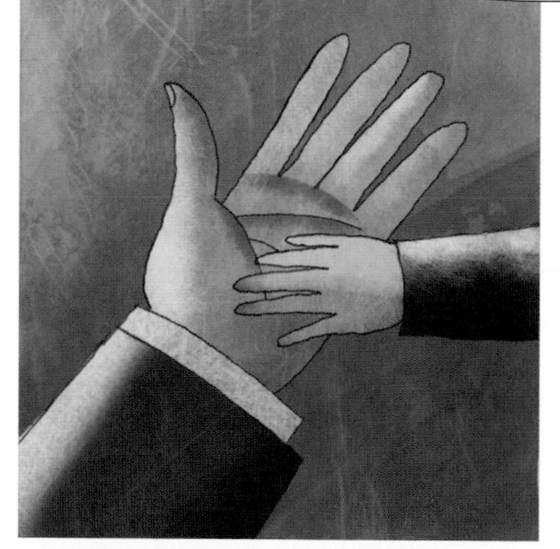
It felt frail.
Yes, it is true.

I'll get you out of the Soviet Union. You'll see Jerusalem.

Zev's face lit up.

Then I told him goodbye.
Zay gezunt.

I started to tell Meyer Gurwitz's wife goodbye too, but she stepped toward Zev and put her arms around him.
She spoke to me softly in Yiddish.
He's a beautiful child, yes?

I knew that no one, no cousin, no postman, no neighbor, had ever called her son beautiful.
Yes, he's very beautiful.

Meyer opened the door and waited for me to step into the narrow hall.
Aren't you afraid to walk with me on the street?

Meyer nodded, his breath quickening, but he walked outside with me along the mud and gravel street.
For a while, neither of us spoke. Then Meyer stopped.

Will you explain to my sister that here in the Soviet Union, the KGB reads everyone's letters? Will you explain to her that after Zev was born, I stopped writing my name and my wife's name in letters for the KGB to read and remember? Will you tell Bela that I think of her and love her very much?
Yes.

And will you explain to her about Zev?
I hesitated.
If I told Bela about her nephew, would she understand why Meyer hid the boy behind a curtain in their one-room apartment?
I'll try.

We were silent again as we walked down the mud street past more rows of gray, wooden buildings.

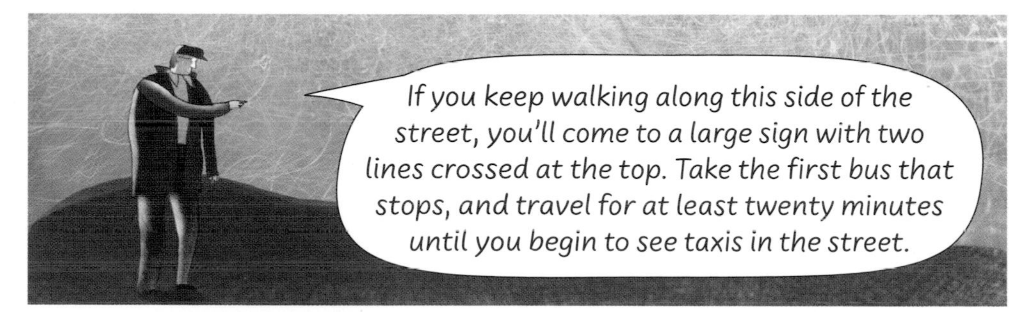
If you keep walking along this side of the street, you'll come to a large sign with two lines crossed at the top. Take the first bus that stops, and travel for at least twenty minutes until you begin to see taxis in the street.

He pulled a torn piece of paper and a short pencil from his pocket.

34

Where are you staying?
The Metropol Hotel.

Show this to the taxi driver and he'll take you to your hotel.
Гостиница
Метрополь

Meyer...

We have congressmen and senators in America. They're the lawmakers of our government. I know several who have influence with your government. I'll go see them. I'll get your family to Israel.

Meyer looked at me a long time.

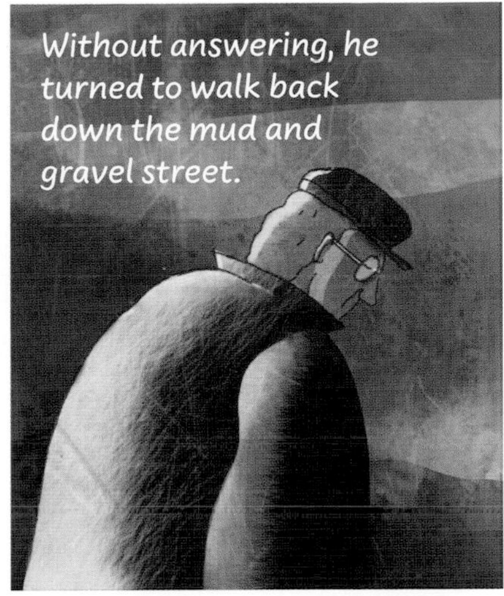

Without answering, he turned to walk back down the mud and gravel street.

At the corner, he stopped and turned around. He barely waved.
35
But for the first time that day, I thought I saw him smile.

He turned again and walked past the rows of gray, wooden buildings to his wife and son.

Zev remembers the rows of gray, wooden buildings in winter. He remembers the building with "35" painted on it. And he remembers a voice speaking in Russian through the door.
35

Is your sister in America a big capitalist?
She must know important politicians because one of them in America is going to get you and your wife visas to leave the USSR.

Zev remembers the voice again.
Open the door just a little. Good rubbish to you. We don't need Jews who keep little boys locked up.
Someone threw in three visas.

He remembers looking down at a river, green trees, green bushes, and in the distance, on the horizon, a city, and then closer, sea and stone, roads, tall buildings, orange roofs in the sun, palm trees, boats.

And later—was it years later? Was he a young man?
He remembers ruins of a rampart on a hill, thick haze over the Hula Valley, soaring birds, and everywhere brown-gray stone, green bushes, blue sky.

He remembers a sudden flash.
A burst of black smoke.
Burning metal.

Over there.

The rabbi puts down the knife.
The room where he sits grows dim.

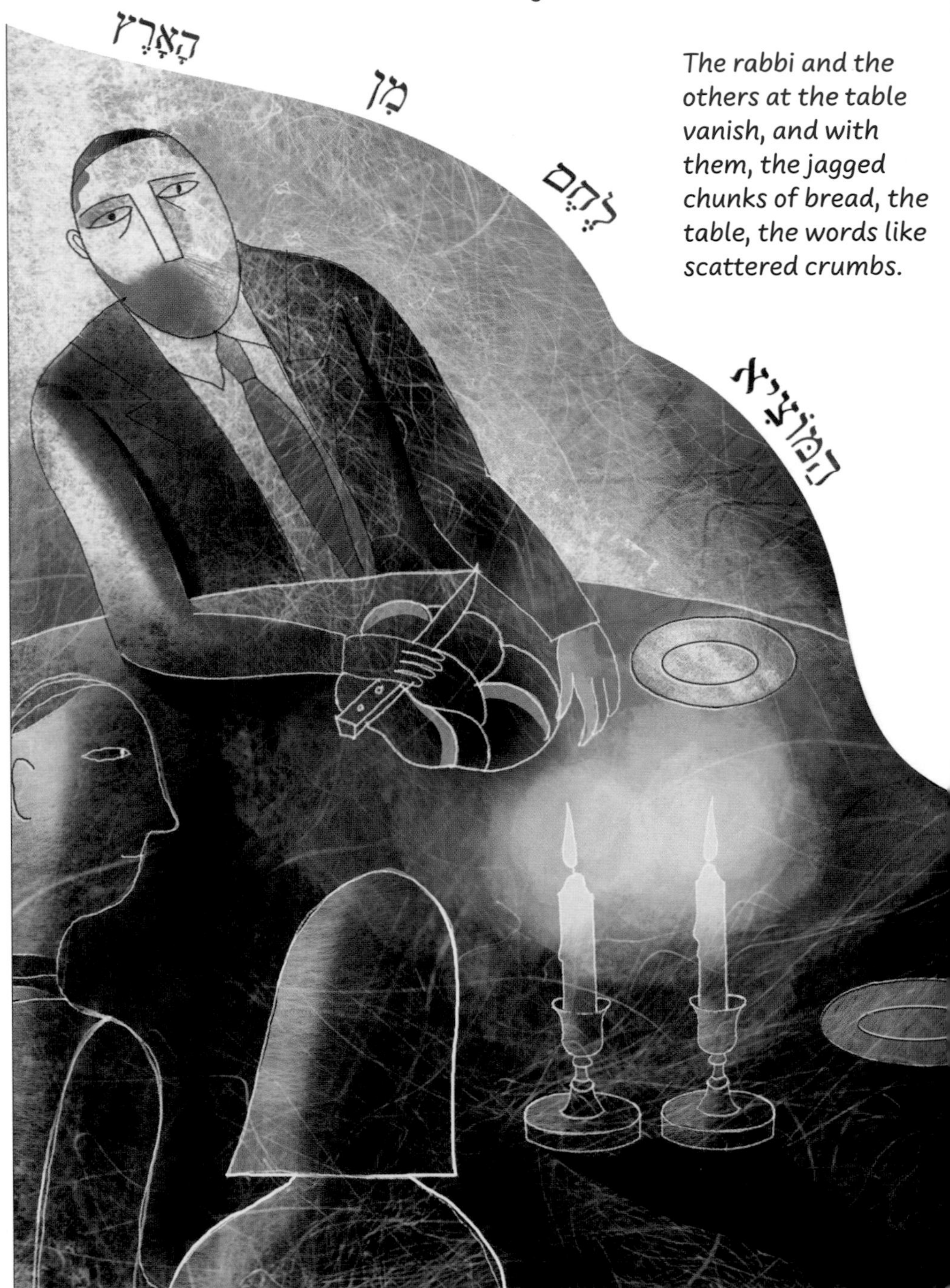

The rabbi and the others at the table vanish, and with them, the jagged chunks of bread, the table, the words like scattered crumbs.

Zev looks around. Left, then right.
Now he remembers. Jagged chunks of bread, scattered crumbs.

White birds, blue sky.

He remembers everything: his own wife, his own children.
Friday nights when he blessed the Sabbath bread and cut it, chunks spreading out in front of him.

He remembers meeting the rabbi again, visiting him at his hotel, sitting at his Sabbath table in a hotel dining room.

He remembers being alive.

He remembers being alive was like being in heaven.
And then.

Afterword

by Hillel Grossman

It has been over fifty years since my father had joined a small group of rabbis to travel to the Soviet Union to meet Jews there and learn about their plight. He came back from the Soviet Union and spoke incessantly about it: to congregants, to local reporters, to the *New York Times*, to congressional representatives and senators. He spoke from the pulpit, at Sisterhood meetings, Men's Club breakfasts, and ecumenical prayer groups. In retrospect, it is remarkable how his talking and that of other intrepid individuals stirred a movement into being, how old were joined by young, both catapulted by the cultural upheavals and the eager and revolutionary zeitgeist of the late 1960s and 1970s. They revealed the chinks in the Iron Wall of the Soviet Union—that the Soviets cared about reputation and public opinion (and of course wheat imports)—which ultimately led to their downfall. My father and others talked the Soviet Union into oblivion.

In his speeches, my father portrayed a vivid picture of stark contrasts: good versus evil, the Jews versus their oppressors, democracy versus demagoguery. But more compelling to him than any of this was the story of individual suffering. His storytelling did not end with the fall of the Soviet Union since the story of individual suffering never ended. Here is where he drew his sense of urgency, and it is what he conveyed so intensely through stories like the one in this book. The story of a child and his parents in a single room with a curtain is one he told over and over. Of his trip to the USSR, my only childhood recollections are of the wait for his return at the JFK international terminal and the gifts he brought for us children: nesting matryoshka and stuffed babushka dolls for my sisters, a fur Cossack hat for me. When we were a bit older, however, we would pull out the metal briefcase of his slides and he would point out the Russian tour guide whose tall beehive hid an embedded recorder, the picture of the old Moscovite rabbi trembling in fear, the young Russian activists who brazenly sang Hatikvah with him.

But the boy behind the curtain was the story that stayed with me. I heard it in sermons, at rallies, at kumsitz campfires, for teenagers in NCSY, Bnai Brith Youth, and at the college Hillel. The details of the story stayed constant, but the denouement evolved as the child grew into a man and my father followed his life course. It was for him the story of devotion, sacrifice, and the never-ending challenge of living a just and meaningful life amidst the harshness of human cruelty. And always there was the looming potential for redemption. It was a story of its time and ours.

A Saga of Soviet Jewry

by Rabbi Aaron Rakeffet-Rothkoff, author of *The Rav: The World of Rabbi Joseph B. Soloveitchik* and *From Washington Avenue to Washington Street*

In 1948 Golda Meir, Israel's first ambassador to the Soviet Union, arrived at the Choral Synagogue in Moscow. Tens of thousands of Jews came out to wave and chant her name. But that show of pro-Israel feeling made Joseph Stalin, the dictator of the Soviet Union, go ballistic. He subsequently instituted repressive policies and purges against the Jews, including the execution of Jewish writers, actors, doctors, and teachers of Jewish religion.

Following Stalin's death in 1953, there was a slight thaw in the Communist attitude toward the Jews. Three years later, a Rabbinical Council of America delegation was allowed to visit the Soviet Union. Despite what the Kremlin tried to present, reports emerged and Jewish activists throughout the world learned about the crisis faced by the millions of Jews living behind the Iron Curtain. Jews were being exiled to Siberia or jailed for trying to teach Torah. Synagogues and yeshivot were outlawed. Soviet Jewish relations with Israel were obstructed. In 1964, the Student Struggle for Soviet Jewry was launched in New York City. With the SSSJ leading the way, groups all over America sprang up to aid and support Soviet Jewry's rights and freedoms.

In an effort to control public opinion, the Kremlin allowed another Rabbinical Council of America delegation to visit in 1965. Rabbi Rafael Grossman, then the spiritual leader of a congregation in Long Branch, New Jersey, was a member of that delegation. Like the other rabbis in the group, he was chosen because of his family's East European roots, his understanding of Jewish affairs, and his ability to speak Yiddish. Rabbi Grossman and the other rabbis knew they were taking risks. The KGB could decide at any moment to arrest them or throw them out of the country. They could be beaten up on the street by KGB hooligans. They would be watched, followed, their luggage searched when they left their hotel and their belongings clearly rifled through—a message that the KGB was on to them.

But Rabbi Grossman and his group took those risks because they wanted to help their fellow Jews in the Soviet Union.

Together with my wife, I spent many months behind the Iron Curtain in the 1980s on behalf of Soviet Jewry. I also took some of the same risks. I soon learned that you cannot help everyone on a personal level, but somehow, there's always some family you will strike up a unique relationship with. That is what happened with Rabbi Grossman and the family portrayed in this book. The saga of Soviet Jewry coming back to its Jewish identity, a saga that included this family, is one of the great achievements of the Jewish nation in modern times.

From the Illustrator's Sketchbook

Although the events of *A Visit to Moscow* are set before my time, the overall spirit of the Soviet Union feels very similar to what it was throughout my childhood when I lived there. I didn't have to make a big leap to connect to the time period.

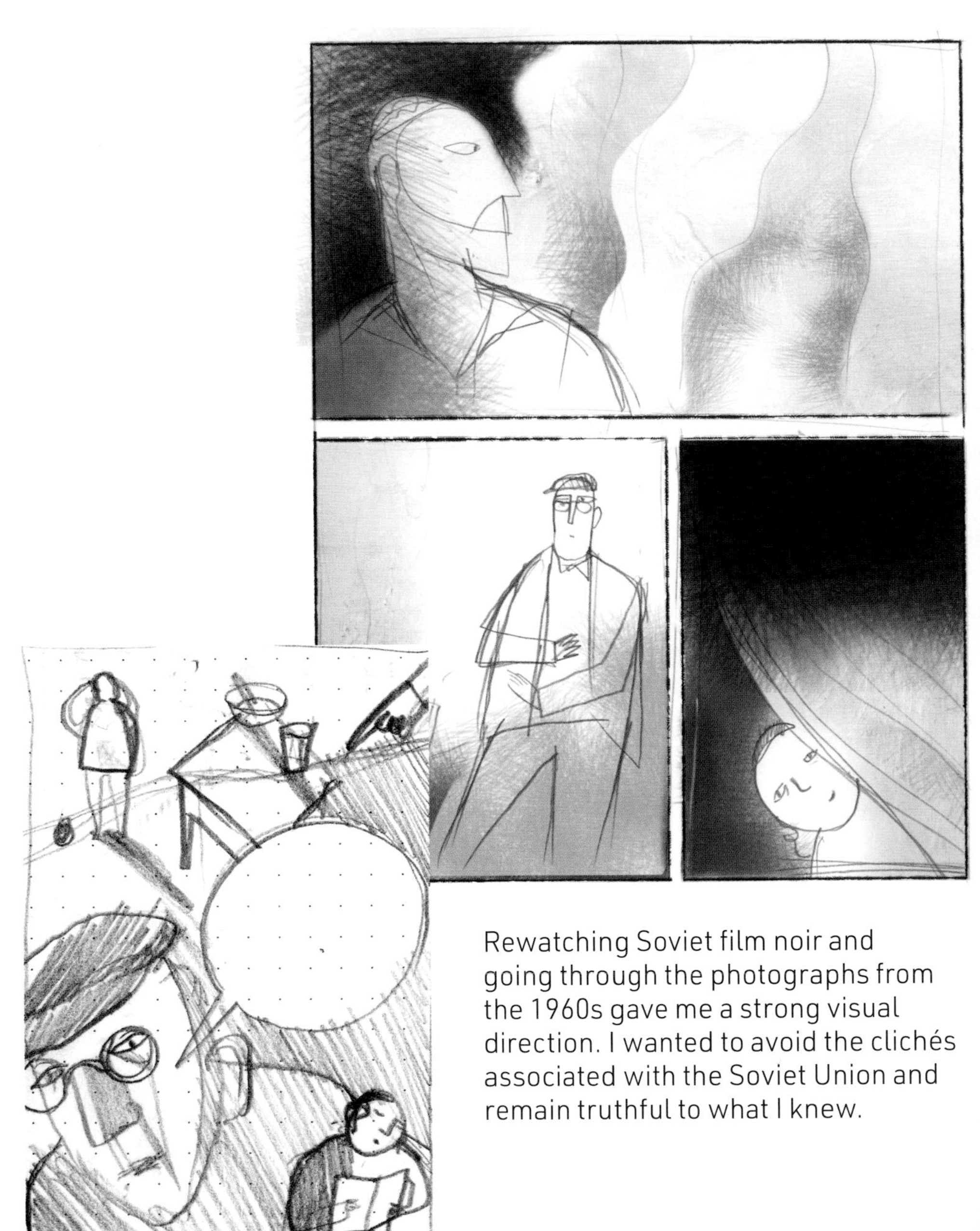

Rewatching Soviet film noir and going through the photographs from the 1960s gave me a strong visual direction. I wanted to avoid the clichés associated with the Soviet Union and remain truthful to what I knew.

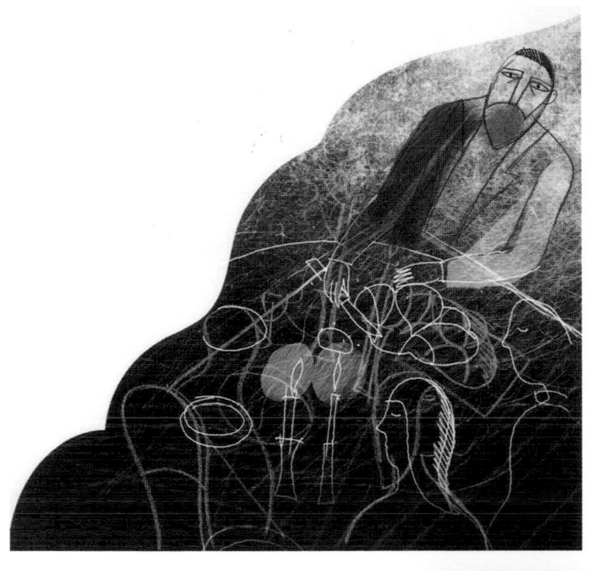

It was an interesting challenge to view the world so familiar to me through the eyes of the American rabbi.

Despite the dread and fear, I could not help but see glimpses of beauty in it.

A Note from the Author

Rabbi Rafael Grossman and I began collaborating on writing projects in the early 1980s. One of our first projects was a Holocaust novel with a character based on his cousin, a leader of the Jewish resistance in the Bialystok ghetto. As we planned out the storyline, Rabbi Grossman told me about an incident during a trip he made in 1965 to the Soviet Union, where he met a young boy whose parents were Holocaust survivors. The boy had never been outside the room he was born in. We included the incident in the book and got about a hundred pages in before the rabbi's articles for a national newspaper became our priority.

We never finished the novel, and then in 2018 Rabbi Grossman died.

I hadn't thought about the manuscript for years until his daughter sent me a box of the writings he and I had once worked on. There, in the box, were the hundred pages of the novel. I dug out the notes from my own files. As I read through them, I realized that along the way I had lost the thread of what had really happened and what we had come up with for the storyline. Was I reading fact or fiction in my notes?

Because of my uncertainty, I knew it wasn't possible to publish the incident of the boy as nonfiction, but what *was* possible? My editor suggested that I write it as historical fiction.

That is how we went forward with *A Visit to Moscow*—"Adapted by Anna Olswanger from a story told by Rabbi Rafael Grossman." The details may never be clear, as evidenced by articles in the *New York Times*, *New York Post*, and Rabbi Grossman's local newspaper *The Daily Record*, which documented the actual trip to the Soviet Union. This is from one of those articles:

> *"My words are guarded. I cannot tell you everything," Rabbi Grossman added as he discussed his tour which he said was taken to "manifest our solidarity and meet with our brethren in that part of the world."*

Was he referring to the boy who had never been outside the room he was born in? Despite my uncertainty, I still sense a truthfulness to the story. Someday I hope to discover the boy's name and where in Israel his family is living. I would like to share *A Visit to Moscow* with them and tell the boy's children how much I admired their father and grandparents for withstanding Soviet repression and for trusting in Rabbi Grossman.

I would like to ask them what was fact and what was fiction.

About the Contributors

RABBI RAFAEL GROSSMAN traveled with eight other rabbis to the Soviet Union in 1965 to visit Jewish victims of government-sponsored anti-Semitism. He met Zev (not his real name) and his parents during that visit.

With the help of Congressmen James Howard and Emanuel Celler, and Senator Clifford Chase, Rabbi Grossman was able to get the "Gurwitz" family to Israel seven years before the Brezhnev-Kosygin government granted the first exit visas to Soviet Jews.

For over twenty-five years Rabbi Grossman visited Zev and his family in Israel. He saw them together for the last time in 1992, the year Zev died at the age of thirty-seven, a husband and father, while on reserve duty with his army unit in Lebanon.

Rabbi Grossman remembered Zev vividly: "When I met him in the Soviet Union, I wondered if he were the victim of both anti-Semitism and religious fanaticism. But when I saw how deeply his parents loved him, I came to believe that the entire family had a strength beyond my understanding. Every time I visited Zev in Israel, he was smiling."

Rabbi Grossman died in Jerusalem in 2018.

ANNA OLSWANGER first began interviewing Rabbi Rafael Grossman and writing down his stories in the early 1980s. She is the author of the middle grade novel *Greenhorn*, based on an incident in Rabbi Grossman's childhood and set against the backdrop of the Holocaust. She is also the author of *Shlemiel Crooks*, a Sydney Taylor Honor Book and PJ Library Book, which she wrote after discovering a 1919 Yiddish newspaper article about the attempted robbery of her great-grandparents' kosher liquor store in St. Louis.

Anna lives in New Jersey with her husband. She is a literary agent and represents a number of award-winning authors and illustrators. Visit her at www.olswanger.com.

YEVGENIA NAYBERG is an award-winning illustrator, painter, and set and costume designer. As a designer, she has been the recipient of numerous awards, including the National Endowment for the Arts/TCG Fellowship for Theatre Designers, the Independent Theatre Award, and the Arlin Meyer Award. She has received multiple awards for her picture book illustrations, including two Sydney Taylor Medals. Her debut author/illustrator picture book, *Anya's Secret Society*, received a Junior Library Guild Gold Selection Award. Her artwork can be found in magazines and on posters and music albums. Originally from Kiev, Ukraine, Yevgenia now lives and draws from her studio in New York City. Visit her at www.nayberg.org

A slide taken of Rabbi Grossman during his trip to the Soviet Union in July, 1965, standing here in front of Peterhof Palace in what was then called Leningrad.